TIRAMISU AND TURMOIL

A BELLE HARBOR COZY MYSTERY (BOOK 5)

SUE HOLLOWELL

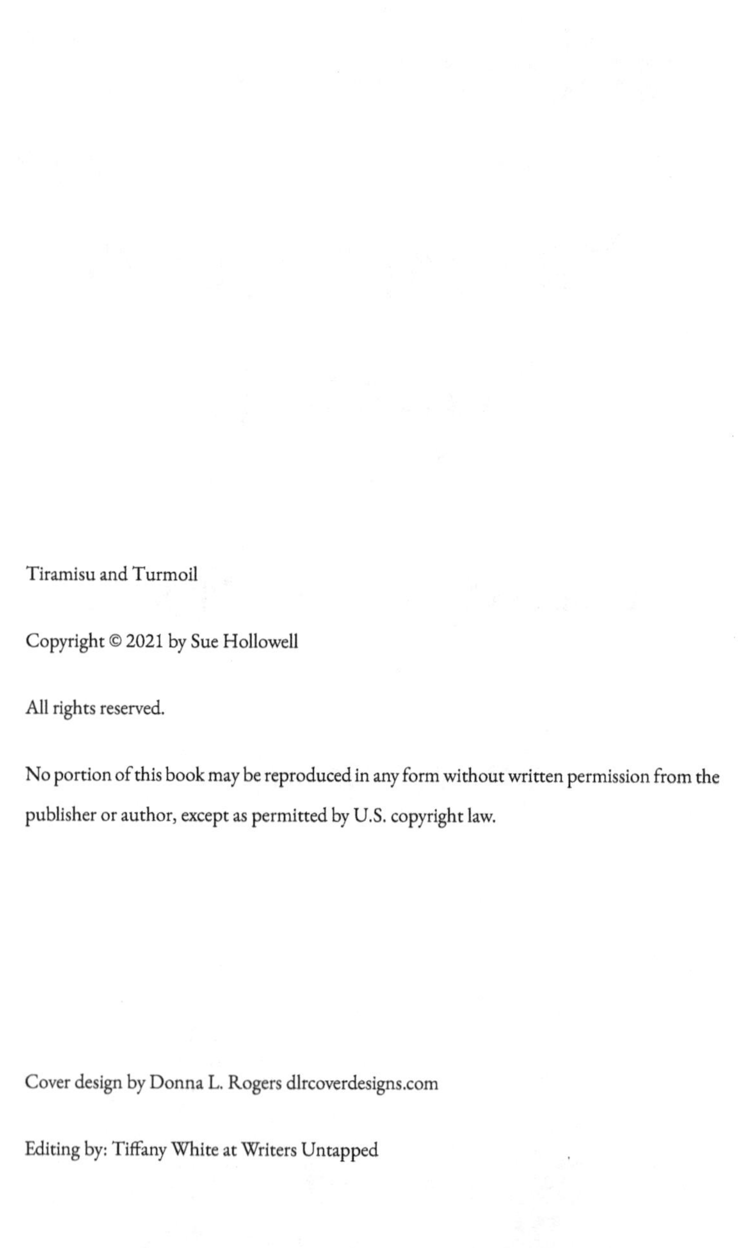

CONTENTS

CHAPTER ONE

"Oh, Tilly," Linda whispered. "I'm so excited for our first collaboration."

"Me too," I whispered back.

Chef Ricardo sneered over the top of his glasses in our direction. Somehow we were going to need to figure out a way to co-exist in this space while we each prepared our food. The chef's reputation preceded him. His food was top notch. His attitude wasn't. When my friend Fiona told me he would be catering the food for the wedding, my stomach dropped to my feet. I knew sharing the kitchen with him would be a challenge. Linda and I didn't need much room to make our tiramisu cheesecake. But any invasion in his arena was unwelcome. His minions were busy chopping, mincing, and whatever else they were doing for their food prep while he barked orders over their shoulders, his chef hat bobbing with every word he spewed. Each time he let loose with a yell, his employees jumped. I only hoped they didn't lose a finger in the process.

Linda and I had set up our workspace on a long counter as far away from the chef as possible. Thankfully our cheesecake recipe didn't need to be baked, but it did require time to cool in the refrigerator to allow it to properly set. I looked at my watch. Plenty of time.

The wedding party and guests had milled about the large mansion in preparation for the wedding. I had counted about fifty people in all joining the festivities. When Fiona told me she had recommended me to her cousin's friend to prepare the desserts, I was sure I wouldn't be hired. Little ol' me and my fledgling bakery. Then Fiona told me the bride was an up-and-coming actress, and I secretly hoped I didn't get the job. How could I be ready for prime time?

With Fiona's insistence, Layla, the bride, gave me a chance with a tasting of dessert samples. I must have made dozens of batches of different things to find a few I thought were worthy of a wedding. Thankfully my tiramisu cheesecake was a winner. Truth be told, it wasn't actually as difficult as the taste would have you believe.

Linda and I continued unpacking and organizing our supplies amid the furtive glances from the chef. He grabbed a tray from one of his staff and held it high. "That's what I'm talking about!" He handed it off to a server who would distribute the snacks to the guests while they waited for the ceremony to begin.

One side of the kitchen was a wall of windows facing the ocean. Outside, an expansive deck ran the length of the house. This place must have been ten times the size of my cottage, but I wouldn't trade my place for the world. It had become my home after moving to Belle Harbor and my little cocoon away from the world. And with my newly adopted little kitten, it was an incredible sanctuary.

"You're not doing it right," came the powerful voice from the other side of the kitchen.

Linda and I looked at each other and shrugged. How could someone function properly under those conditions? I put my hand on her arm as she retrieved the mascarpone from the bag. I smiled, then glanced at Ricardo and back at Linda. "I'm so glad you agreed to become my assistant."

She put the cheese on the counter and squeezed me in a tight hug. Releasing me, she looked directly into my eyes. "You did me a favor. I feel like I've been given a new life. After my husband died, I rattled around that big house, unsure what to do with myself. Thank you," Linda said.

"Quiet!" Chef Ricardo bellowed.

Linda put her hand over her mouth and dipped her head, snickering. My eyes widened, hoping her gesture didn't get us banished from the kitchen.

We started with step one and prepared the pans and the crust for the cheesecake. Silently, we worked in perfect rhythm together. Linda placed parchment paper into the springform pans and greased them. She took some of the ingredients to the refrigerator and returned to our work counter.

Ricardo whipped his head in our direction.

"We agreed. Two shelves in the cooler," I boldly stated. My hands shook as I finished mixing the ingredients for the crusts. With a million times more confidence than I felt, I stood tall and returned to my task, hearing nothing more from Ricardo. OK, battle number one went to the ladies. I didn't want to intentionally tick him off, but I wasn't going to cower either.

"Tilly," Linda started, glancing at Ricardo. She lowered her voice. Might as well not tempt the troll. "You told me you had an idea for your bakery location." We each took mounds of the cookie crust and pressed it into the pans. I couldn't believe how lucky I got at finding Linda to join me as an assistant in the bakery. Or maybe the universe had guided us together. I had met her when Uncle Jack agreed to run her estate sale, something he hadn't done in quite a while. She was perfect for me... and I think perfect for Unkie. Things were moving along well between the two of them. It was adorable to see them flirt with each other like teenagers. My uncle was perennially happy, but Linda catapulted his mood into the atmosphere.

"Yes. With Poppy's Pizza Parlor going out of business, I got to thinking that might be an option. I'm going to look at it later with the realtor and see what work it might need," I said.

This move would be incredibly bittersweet. Uncle Jack had carved out a space in the corner of his Checkered Past Antique store for my little baking kitchen. Leaving that location meant my business was doing well, everything I wanted. But not seeing my uncle as much weighed heavy on my heart. I secretly wondered if there was a place big enough for both of us to move to. But the location he had on the beach for his store had been his space for over forty years.

Before my Uncle Frank passed, the two of them had been unstoppable. Unkie had lost his step for a while after his brother's death, but my arrival in town seemed to get him out of his funk and give him new life. I didn't want to hurt that, but he was the first to encourage me to get my own space. We would just have to develop a new routine together. Poppy's Pizza wasn't too far from the antique store, so I was sure we could find a way to make it work.

Several people ran by the kitchen, going from the front of the house to the back. The voices raised significantly, and yelling started. I couldn't make out the words. Chef Ricardo's team stopped what they were doing and all heads swiveled toward the commotion.

He raised his arms in the air, screaming, "Did I tell you to stop?" Sheepishly, they all obediently returned to their tasks. The chef stomped over to Linda and me and asked, "What's going on?"

Several more people filed by the door, a few sniffling. "I can't believe this is happening," one of them said.

I turned to Linda, my eyes wide. I stuck my head into the hallway as the entire crowd streamed past. "The wedding is off" I heard as everyone moved toward the great room of the house.

Pots and pans were clanging behind me as Chef Ricardo slammed them into the sink, some full of food. "I knew it. That entitled little brat. Who would want to marry her anyway?"

I looked at my watch and saw I had a few minutes before the cheesecake crusts needed to get into the cooler. If we even needed them anymore. Curiosity got the best of me and I joined the throng.

CHAPTER TWO

The momentum of the crowd carried me down the hallway from the kitchen to the great room. From behind, a nudge moved me to the side.

The wedding photographer shuffled past me. "Sorry," he said as he went by. He continued excusing himself through the crowd to get to the point of the pandemonium.

Most of the group milled about with murmurs, fingers pointing and eyes averted. Like one of those scenes you don't want to see but can't look away from. Intense crying emerged from the room on the side, where it appeared the groom had been getting ready for the wedding. The photographer entered the room and raised his camera.

"What are you doing?" a gruff voice said as the man grabbed the photographer by the arm.

Reeling off several snaps of the camera, the photographer jerked his arm from the man. "I'm doing my job," he said and stepped closer to the body.

"Tilly," came a whisper from behind me. I jumped and my heartbeat accelerated. I put my hand on my chest and turned to see Fiona. She clutched my elbow and ushered me to the side of the room. We stood near the wall of windows overlooking the ocean. Any other day, this setting would be a magical place for a wedding. The scenery unmatched in its beauty. And the vantage point up on the hill provided a one hundred eighty degree view of the beach. The weather was, as usual, perfect in Belle Harbor. The sun glistening off the water belied the gloomy mood of the house.

Fiona and I hugged a wall toward a corner of the room. "What's going on?" I asked.

She shook her head. If it wasn't for Fiona, I wouldn't be here for my most illustrious job since starting my bakery. "When I passed by the room, I saw Aiden on the floor with a pool of blood. It doesn't look good." She closed her eyes.

"What could have happened?" I asked. The crowd had now gathered into a few distinct groups, which appeared to be separated by those on the side of the groom from those with the bride.

"She's my friend," the photographer yelled at the man trying to steer him from the room.

"My daughter doesn't need you bothering her during this difficult time." The father of the bride returned to the room with the groom. With the parting of the crowd I saw the groom splayed on the floor, not moving. Fiona was spot on. Nobody attempted help, leaving me to conclude he was dead.

The photographer huffed around the room, stopping next to Fiona and me, apparently thinking we were a more friendly audience.

"Brody, what happened?" Fiona asked.

He pulled out his camera and showed us one of the pictures he was able to get before he was ousted from the room. We huddled around the small screen as he enlarged it for us to view. The groom looked like he was napping on the floor. Fully dressed and ready for the wedding, boutonniere and all. Brody looked back and forth between Fiona and me. "I'm not sorry to say I'm glad he's gone. She was too good for him," he said and snapped the cover onto the camera lens.

I raised my eyebrows at Fiona. Maybe all was not well in paradise. The bride and groom were both up-and-coming actors. When Fiona pitched me to make the desserts for the affair, I questioned whether I wanted to be a part of something so visible. After discussing with Linda and Uncle Jack, I decided I couldn't afford to turn down business. And the upside from the publicity could be tremendous, if things went well. Now, I wondered how this would play out.

Brody continued his semi-rant. "I told her from the beginning he was riding her coattails." He sighed and stepped to the window, gazing out toward the water. "He was so jealous that she got the lead in that blockbuster *Strangers of Everywhere*. He couldn't just be happy for her."

Fiona moved to Brody's side. "What are you saying?" she asked.

I glanced toward the room with the body. The bride was on her knees, her head laying on Aiden's chest, her body heaving in sobs. What was the etiquette at a time like this? I hoped Linda had everything under control in the kitchen. I peeked at my watch. The crusts were done by now and she was probably making the filling. I was torn between staying to learn more about what happened or returning to the job I was hired to do.

"I'm not sure," Brody answered. "I'm just upset, as we all are." He removed his lens cap, turned, and began snapping pics again. I wasn't sure what the purpose was, given there would be no wedding today. And many would prefer not to memorialize this event.

"Brody," Fiona admonished him.

"OK. Sorry, it's instinct. I'll just put it away so I'm not tempted." He stashed his camera inside the large carrying case hanging from his shoulder.

"Oh, Brody. I can't believe he's gone," a younger woman wailed as she approached and fell into Brody's arms. He enveloped her and patted her back as she gasped for breath. From her dress, she appeared to be a bridesmaid. The A-line V-neck floor-length dress in navy swooshed as she moved.

Fiona pulled a tissue from her purse and handed it to the woman.

"Thank you." She held out her arm to steady herself on a nearby chair, plopping into it. She bent forward, continuing to weep. The tendrils from her dark brown hair escaped their clasp and gently swayed as she cried.

Brody knelt next to her, his hand on her shoulder. "Emma, I'm sorry," he said.

Emma lifted her head, wiping her nose with the tissue. She fiddled with it in her hands. "How is Layla ever going to get over this? He was the love of her life," she whimpered.

Brody looked at us and slightly shook his head. "She's going to need you to support her," he said.

Emma stood. "I know." She handed Brody the tissue, straightened her dress, and kissed him on the cheek, leaving a bright red outline of lips. Emma strode away, putting on a good face for her friend.

"Well, she can certainly turn her emotions on a dime," Fiona said.

Brody jammed the tissue into his pocket. "Yeah, she's a pretty good actress in her own right."

I stepped forward. "Fiona, I should probably get back to the kitchen to help Linda. I don't know what they're going to want to do about eating, but I suspect we'll all be here for a while, and I want to be prepared."

The crowd continued to mumble as I wound my way through the group to return to the kitchen. I overheard statements of sorrow, sympathy, and accusations of wrongdoing. The finger pointing had started, blame going around all sides, the bride's and groom's families lining up against each other to stake out their positions.

Barney would have his hands full with this crowd. I only hoped he could discern the acting from the real deal.

CHAPTER THREE

From down the hallway I could hear Chef Ricardo banging pots and pans and yelling. I hoped Linda had survived my absence. Gulping, I headed that way, bracing for the storm.

"Tilly," Barney said as he and his deputy appeared at the other end of the hall. He had his hat in his hand, his jowls sagging. I stopped as they approached.

The sound of shattering glass came from the direction of the kitchen. We all whipped our heads, Barney taking a step toward the clatter. I placed my hand on his arm, shaking my head.

"That's just the temperamental chef," I whispered and pointed to the opposite end, indicating what Barney was looking for was behind me.

"Are you sure?" Barney asked. "It doesn't sound good in there." He turned toward the kitchen again.

I nodded and pivoted, retracing my steps, leading them toward the crowd. The chef was the least of our concern. The low rumbles from the gathering got increasingly louder as we approached.

At the opening to the great room, Fiona met us and said, "I'm glad you're here. They're getting pretty restless."

Barney looked over Fiona's shoulder, scanning the room. He stepped forward, bellowing, "OK everyone."

Most sounds immediately stopped. Several heads swiveled toward the room with the groom. Barney looked to his right, his gaze stopping when he spotted the body.

"Chief, I'll go take a look," the deputy said. All eyes followed his movements.

Barney moved to the middle of the room, drawing the attention of everyone away from Aiden. "I'm sorry this has happened. But we're going to need to gather some information," he said.

"You should start with Cooper," someone mumbled.

"Hey," Cooper yelled, looking for the source of the accusation.

Barney held up his hand. "We'll be talking with each of you. I'd like to keep this orderly and civil. In the meantime, the chef is preparing food so you'll have something to eat." Barney raised his eyebrows toward me, appearing to seek confirmation of his statement.

"Yes, we'll let everyone know when it's ready," I responded, hoping I didn't commit the testy chef to something beyond his wishes.

Barney continued his movements to distance himself from the obvious center of attention: Aiden lying dead just a few feet away. "Let's get settled in for the time being. Deputy Stevens and I will be interviewing you in groups." He directed the bride and bridesmaids to return to the bridal suite.

Layla place her arm on her forehead. "Will this nightmare ever end?" she wailed. Emma put her arm around Layla's waist, picked up the train from Layla's wedding dress, and guided her away.

Cooper rushed to Layla's side, leaning close to her. "We'll get to the bottom of this. Hang in there," he said, his voice cracking.

Emma hugged Layla tighter and pulled away.

Barney continued to peel off the different groups, ordering them to their assigned locations.

"My baby will never recover from this. That full-of-himself guy was never good enough for my Layla." A large man in a tux waved his arms around, as dramatic as his daughter.

"OK, sir. I'm going to need you and your family to head upstairs. Don't worry. We'll sort this out," Barney said. He followed the man toward the hallway to ensure he complied with his instructions. The man was followed by several people, all supportive of the bride.

Barney turned and moved toward the groomsmen, all adorned in identical navy tuxes, matching vests, bright white shirts, and black shoes. If you didn't know any better, you would think they were about to break out into a barbershop four-part harmony. "You four, I want you in the room on the other side of the bridal suite," Barney said. He escorted them past the room with Aiden to the end of the great room opening into the desired destination.

That left the groom's family and friends huddling in a corner. Barney looked around and tapped his chin.

I stepped forward and said, "Maybe outside on the deck. There's lots of room out there."

Barney held up a finger. "Yes." He approached the group and gently said, "Again, I'm so sorry. Please head out to the deck for now. I will keep you posted."

The group nodded assent and silently went through the sliding door to the deck, single file. The cool ocean air rushed inside, giving oxygen to the room where it had all been used up. Closing the door behind the group, Barney turned and sighed.

With the great room vacant, he headed to see the body. "That's sure a lot of drama. I mean, a dead body will do that. But they are a bit over the top," Barney said.

"I might have left out the part about how several of the people here are professional actors," I said.

Barney raised his arms. "Yes, that might have been helpful to know." He entered the room with the groom, circling the body. Aiden lay there in his tux, his curly blond hair slightly moussed, his arms out to his side like he had just settled in for a nap.

Barney crouched. "Hmmm," he said. "What do you think?"

"Well, I—" I started.

"Um," Deputy Stevens said. "I think he means me."

My face warmed. Of course he did.

"Well, Chief, first, I'm seeing no signs of trauma that would explain the blood. Unless that happened when he fell," Deputy Stevens offered.

Click. Click. Click.

"Are you kidding me?" Barney stood and stepped toward Brody.

"I just thought you might—" Brody backed up, realizing he was about to be admonished.

Barney reached out his hand. "Let me see that," he said.

Brody retreated further, looking toward me for guidance.

I shrugged. Barney was in charge. And if he wanted to see the camera, why not. "Maybe you have something that could be a clue." I placed my hand on Brody's back and nudged him forward.

Brody dropped the camera bag on the floor and turned the camera screen toward Barney, scrolling through the pictures.

Barney looked up at him. "I may need to see those later. Nothing stands out right now as obvious. But there's got to be an explanation. Don't go far." Barney circled Aiden like he was willing a clue to jump out at him.

"Tilly," Fiona whispered to me.

Barney lifted his arm and pointed to the door. "Alright, the three of you. Out," he said and ushered us from the room. "I really need you to make sure the food is on its way. There's no better way to calm people and keep them occupied than to feed them. And if I know you, Tilly, you've got a fabulous dessert to treat everyone."

Fiona linked arms with me and waved Brody our direction. We silently exited, closing the door behind us. I was still in shock that the wedding of the century, with all of the beauty surrounding us, had been marred with a murder. While we had waited for Barney to arrive, I scanned the crowd to imagine each guest as the killer. I couldn't fathom which of them would do such a thing. Everyone all dressed up in their fancy clothes. And why would you choose to do it at a wedding? I guess if it was the last attempt to keep Layla and Aiden apart, a desperate person wouldn't be thinking clearly. But who could that be?

As we neared the kitchen, the clanging had reduced to a dull roar. I only hoped the food preparations had sufficiently progressed to quickly start serving food.

CHAPTER FOUR

We rounded the corner to enter the kitchen. I braced myself for a barrage of words from the chef and his team.

Chef Ricardo jerked his head our direction as we arrived. He stomped over and held his finger within a few inches of my face. "Tell me that the show is still going on," he said. His gaze darted between Fiona, Brody, and me, waiting for confirmation to his order.

I nodded. "Obviously the wedding is off. But the chief wants us to finish preparing and serving food to the guests to keep them occupied."

The chef's shoulders dropped. He wiped his arm across his forehead. "Of course. And who would want to miss my exquisite creations under any circumstances." He whipped around and strutted back to his crew with all of the arrogance he could muster. I wondered if I would be that confident in my food one day. Chef Ricardo resumed his directing, arms moving like a music conductor.

I covered my nose with my hand and glanced at Fiona. She wrinkled her nose in acknowledgment. The place stunk like rotten fish. I saw the assembly line of plates ready to receive the food. A large baking pan held several pieces of fish seasoned with spices. The chef was scooping one piece per plate. I hoped it tasted much better than it smelled. How could he not realize there was an issue? But keeping him focused on his task was the best way to keep the peace.

Linda was busy on the left side of the kitchen, as far away from the chef's antics as possible. She had prepared the cheesecake filling and the cakes were being refrigerated before the final step of adding the Kahlua whipped cream. Linda and I had searched far and wide to find a unique cheesecake recipe that did not require baking. There wouldn't have been time to do that here and we would have had to prepare them the night before. Her head was bowed over the mixing bowl.

"Linda, how is it going? What can I do?" I asked. I stepped to the counter. The mixer was on high speed for the topping, the requisite peaks forming nicely. She turned it off and stepped over to me, glancing at the chef.

With her voice low, she said, "When Chef Ricardo is about to serve, we can plate up the desserts." Linda had the kitchen well under control, including the excitable chef. I had to hand it to my new assistant. When we took this catering job, I thought it would be the two of us partnering together. The drama was now at a whole other level.

Chef Ricardo had finished dishing up the fish. He began instructing his team to assemble the salads. From my vantage point, they were a masterpiece. With the white plates as a background, the colors popped. Green leaves, yellow sliced bell peppers, and bright red miniature watermelon slices. If nothing else, his food looked incredible, like a work of art. The chef took two steps back and crossed his arms, tipping his head. "Yes, just perfect," he said.

Linda grabbed a stack of dessert plates and lined several of them in a row on the counter. "What's going on out there?" Linda asked.

The chef turned around and gave us the evil eye.

Linda held out her arm toward him. "You're doing an amazing job, especially under these difficult and very trying conditions," she said.

He nodded and returned to finish the salad construction.

"You are a magician," I said to her, snickering. No wonder the kitchen had continued to function. Linda had a gentle, guiding touch with persnickety personalities. Another reason she was a great assistant. Sometimes you get difficult customers. There didn't seem to be much she couldn't do.

"It looks like the food will be ready soon," Fiona said. "What do you think about also opening the bar early to provide adult beverages to go along with it?"

I shrugged. "Sounds good to me."

The supplies for the bar were located on a cart in the corner of the kitchen. The plan was to open it after the ceremony and after everyone had been served their meal. However, all bets were off today. Probably as long as the guests remained lucid, Barney would be OK with it. And it might even loosen a few tongues to accelerate him getting the information he needed for the investigation.

"Brody, can you help me?" Fiona asked. She turned toward him. "Brody!"

He shook his head, appearing deep in thought, possibly wondering how to keep away from the chef's wrath. "Ummm," he said and followed her.

"Miss Linda." The chef approached her, carrying a large bread knife in his right hand. "How should we go about serving?" he asked.

I could see over his shoulder that his team was pulling fresh-baked bread from the oven. The overwhelming comfort smell overtook the stink of the fish, thankfully. The long loaves smelled of fresh rosemary. He really had concocted a gem of a meal.

I joined Linda and said, "Barney has assigned groups to different rooms. Why don't we serve a room at a time?" I asked.

The chef nodded his approval of the suggestion and returned to slicing bread.

Fiona had Brody preparing pitchers of her Romero and Julieta hibiscus tea cocktail. Ironically, the drink suited the situation of the wedding. Who knew when she chose it we would be dealing with a murder?

Linda retrieved one of the cheesecakes from the refrigerator and removed the edge of the springform pan. She sliced it and placed one section on each plate. I followed her, piping the Kahlua whipped cream on top with a sprinkle of cocoa for garnish. With all plates prepared for our first serving, I said, "I'm going to give Uncle Jack a quick call. He'll be wondering after a while when I'm not there to pick up Peanut."

"Yes, go," Linda said, shooing me away.

I glanced at the chef, deep in conversation with his team. We might just be able to pull this off after all. I stepped into the hallway so as to not disturb the rhythm of the kitchen. Hearing the details of the murder might just send Chef Ricardo off the deep end. To be fair, it was quite disturbing to everyone. But a man with a knife just might become unpredictable.

Looking up and down the corridor, I knew the coast was clear for my call. "Unkie, it's Tilly," I said quietly into my phone, cupping my mouth for as much privacy as I could get. "There's been a bit of a development here, and I wanted to let you know I'll be late." I didn't know much, other than the fact that the groom was murdered. I gave him the lowdown. When news got out, the story would be all over the media. I was just glad it hadn't gotten that far—yet.

Uncle Jack had agreed to babysit our kittens while Linda and I were at the event. The three of us had been blessed to adopt kittens from the litter between our bookstore neighbor's cat, Gwinnie, and Willie, a cat belonging to the tenant living above Uncle Jack's antique store. The theatrics that had ensued when Gwinnie's owner found out she was pregnant by Willie would have rivaled the performances of the actors in attendance at this wedding.

Closing my eyes, I dreamed of returning home and cuddling with my little furball. I thanked Unkie and returned to the sound of breaking glass in the kitchen. What now?

CHAPTER FIVE

"You imbecile!" Chef Ricardo's face was as red as a beet. He stood on tiptoes to reach the height of his sous chef. "You are wasting perfectly good cuisine," he bellowed.

The sous chef muttered, "Sorry, Chef." He bent to scoop up the splattered mess of fish and salad. Bread from the plate had rolled under the counter.

Coming to the rescue, Fiona proffered the chef a glass of her cocktail. "Would you do me the honor and be the first to taste this?" She handed Chef Ricardo a glistening fuchsia liquid in a tall glass with ice and a sprig of rosemary. "I'm hoping it compliments your meal well," she said.

Looking around at his audience, the chef took the glass and put it to his lips. He inhaled and sipped, closing his eyes. "Your elixir is perfect!" The chef swigged a large portion of the drink. "Desperate times call for desperate measures," he said, holding the glass like a lifeline.

No doubt. And Fiona had conjured another winner. "Why don't we start with the drinks? Then you can serve the main meal." Fiona gazed around the room for agreement with her plan. Hearing no dissension, she proceeded to her drink cart. "Tilly." Fiona pointed to a tray with glasses and a bucket of ice. She grabbed her tray with two pitchers of the beautiful beverage.

"Brody, can you help Linda finish with the desserts?" I asked.

He had moved to the window, gazing at who knew what. He didn't acknowledge her.

I stepped beside him and softly touched his arm. "Brody?" I whispered.

Sniffling, he turned toward me, eyes moist. "Who would do this?" he asked.

Shaking my head, I said, "Barney will find out. Rest assured. Fiona and I are going to serve drinks. Can you help Linda while we're gone?"

Brody glanced toward the cheesecake preparation area and shrugged. "I guess. Why would someone want to hurt Layla?" he asked.

Was he confused? Was he in shock? Did he not realize the groom was the one murdered? I guided him to Linda, who took his hand, hoping the distraction of some manual labor would ease his mind.

Fiona and I exited the kitchen, off on our mission. "Let's go upstairs first," I said. We turned left toward the grand entrance of the house. The entryway was large enough that it could have held the guests for the ceremony. We started up the winding staircase, the glasses clinking on the tray. Fiona and I were side by side as we ascended to the top. I wasn't sure where Barney had deposited the bride's family. I only hoped beginning the food and beverage service would keep the calm Barney needed for his investigation.

"Well, that was weird with Brody," Fiona said. "He seemed more upset about Layla than he did Aiden."

We stopped at the top of the stairs, pondering which direction to proceed. I couldn't hear a thing. I tipped my head to the right. "I know. It makes me wonder if there was something going on with him and Layla," I said.

Pausing again to figure out which way to go, we heard mumblings behind the second door to our right. "He did seem very protective of her. And I think he's been following her for some time from his freelance photography days with that rag tabloid magazine. Even from the earliest days of her career."

We stopped outside the door holding our first group of customers. The voices were now loud enough to make out some of the conversation. I felt a bit uneasy listening in, but if it could help Barney, I was willing to do it. Fiona and I leaned in. I heard "Brody" and a reference to slime. There did not appear to be love lost from the bride's family for him, despite his care for their daughter.

"Should we go in?" Fiona mouthed.

I held up one finger from my hand holding the tray, wanting to take every advantage of the opportunity. We might get nothing of use in the investigation. But when people didn't know someone was listening, they might have loose lips. "I need to go find Layla," a man's voice said, probably her father.

"The police said to wait here, Norman," a woman said.

"I can't take this much more," Norman replied. "When this gets out, how is it going to affect her career?"

It sure didn't sound like they cared much about Aiden either. Their future son-in-law was murdered, and they were more worried about the optics for Layla? No more wondering where she got her vanity—it was from dear old dad.

"Norman!" The woman's voiced raised.

"You know he was only bringing her down. If you ask me, this is the best-case scenario," Norman said.

With Layla standing to gain, would her dad have stepped in to stop the marriage? Had he tried to talk Layla out of it previously with no success? Parents had been known to go to the ends of the earth for their kids. Did Norman off Aiden to ensure his daughter's celebrity status continued to rise?

I shook my head. This was beyond belief if it were true. I tapped my knuckle on the door. "Hello, everyone," I said.

Norman yanked the door wide open, gesturing for us to enter. Barney had directed this group to wait in the library. Books lined the walls to both left and right, with several brown leather wing chairs facing the center of the room. Fiona proceeded to the opposite end of the room and put the tray with drink pitchers on a table.

"Thank God!" someone said and met us at the table. Everyone else followed suit and lined up for a drink.

Grabbing a scoop from the ice bucket, I loaded several glasses and began handing them to Fiona. She filled each one and topped it with a sprig of rosemary.

"We're starting off with cocktails. The main meal will be up short-ly," I said. We continued serving until everyone had a drink. The room had quieted, the only sound that of sipping.

"Well, I paid for this. I'm glad to see the caterers aren't planning to slip out," Norman said.

Fiona raised her eyebrows at his comment and pursed her lips. I was pretty sure my friend had a sharp retort to Norman's comment that she was stifling. In any other circumstance, she wouldn't let him get away with that rude statement.

We headed toward the door, leaving the pitchers behind. "It shouldn't be long now. And the chef has prepared an exquisite meal. You are most certainly getting your money's worth," I said.

Norman harrumphed.

I closed the door behind me as we returned to the hallway, Fiona slapping her hand over her mouth.

I grabbed her arm, not sure if I was about to die laughing at my pompous comments or scream at Norman's crass attitude.

We stepped away from the door. "That guy is a piece of work," Fiona said. "I'm sure his daughter is devastated, and all he can think about is fame and money. Disgusting."

We reversed our directions to return to the kitchen for our next delivery. "Well, thanks for holding back. Actually, the word of mouth from this catering gig could bring us more business. For better or worse," I said. We needed to move on to the next group of guests. Who knew what additional details we would discover on our tour of the house?

CHAPTER SIX

Deputy Stevens had his head buried in his notebook as he climbed up the staircase. He raised up his head to greet us, waving. "Hey ladies, how's it going?" he asked.

Fiona and I looked at each other. That was quite the casual, congenial greeting in the middle of a murder mystery investigation. "Umm, there's been a murder? So not great for some of us," Fiona said.

That girl said directly what was on her mind. She raised her palms in a *well, that was a dumb question* kind of way.

Nonplussed, the deputy asked where the bride's family was located. Fiona pointed the direction we had just come from. "Second door on your right. And I'm pretty sure you'll want to talk with the bride's father," she said.

"Oh? Why is that?" he asked, pulling his pencil from his shirt pocket, poised to take notes.

Fiona glanced over her shoulder and leaned forward. "I don't think he wanted the wedding to happen."

The deputy nodded, encouraging Fiona to continue. He took another step to join us on the same level.

"He was upset that the marriage to Aiden would ruin Layla's career," she continued, watching the deputy furiously write in his notebook.

He raised his head. "And?" he prompted.

Fiona looked at me and back at Deputy Stevens. "Isn't that enough? I mean, the rich and famous can think they're untouchable. He might do anything he could for his daughter."

Continuing his ascent of the staircase, he said, "Well, good work. But don't let the chief hear you say you've been snooping. He frowns upon civilians getting involved in our work."

Huffing her way down, Fiona said, "Well, that's a little ungrateful." I followed her as we returned to the kitchen.

We rounded the corner into the busy hive, silent except for rattling of dishes now and then. Everyone had a game face on, focused on their tasks. The drama had simmered, for now.

"Miss Linda." Chef Ricardo approached her as she continued plating the tiramisu cheesecake.

She turned toward him, her smile warm. "Yes, Chef? What can I help you with?" she asked.

He closed his eyes and shook his head. "No, Miss Linda. It's you. I am obliged for your calm in the kitchen. I could learn a lot from you." He took her hand and brushed it with a gentle kiss.

"You're welcome," Linda said. "And I understand your passion for your craft." That woman could have success at hostage negotiations. I wouldn't have believed it if I didn't see it with my own eyes. "Tilly, is the bride's family ready for their meals?"

"In just a few minutes. Deputy Stevens was just arriving upstairs as we were leaving." I looked at Fiona and back at Linda. "Maybe a little longer. I think he might be there a while."

With that news, the chef raised his arm to throw a towel onto the counter. Mid-swing he stopped and smiled at Linda, gently laying the towel down. He breathed in and audibly blew out.

"I can't stay here anymore. The suspense is killing me. I need to go see how Layla is doing." Brody started toward the exit.

Fiona grabbed his arm. "Not so fast," she said.

"But I—" Brody's shoulders slumped. "She's going to need some comfort." His eyes pleaded for Fiona to release him.

The chef had lined up his team with three trays of food. "I cannot wait any longer," he said and marched them from the kitchen. Despite the circumstances, the plates appeared like works of art. Each beautifully designed, almost too good to eat.

We watched them file out, the tension in the room lowering several notches.

"Upstairs and to the right," I hollered after them.

Brody collapsed into one of the chairs at the counter, laying his head in his arms. His body shook with sobs. He tipped his head up, saying, "I knew he wasn't good for her. I just never thought it would end like this." He buried his head, continuing to weep.

Linda approached Brody and placed her hand on his back. "What do you mean?" she whispered. That woman had skills!

Brody sniffed loudly. "I've grown to love Layla. Ever since I started photographing her, I've seen many times how poorly Aiden treated her. I never captured that in my pics. Although, there were times if I had, the price I could have commanded for those would have made me a rich man." He stood and paced. "I tried to help her the best I could." He approached the window and gazed out. The palm trees swayed in the gentle breeze. This event had turned anything but relaxing. "I thought she was starting to care for me too."

Were Layla and Brody in cahoots to kill Aiden? How far would he go to protect her? Would she have used him to get her way, exit from the marriage before it even started? That way she could be seen as the grieving fiancée. Who would expect her to be involved in his death?

"Brody, is there something you need to tell us?" Linda asked.

He whipped his head around, eyes wide. "What? I had nothing to do with this." He stepped forward, his arms out, pleading his case.

"What about Layla?" Linda went right to the heart of the matter. If she wasn't careful, she would be solving the crime for Barney. I watched the interaction between the two of them, eager to hear the response.

Brody looked at me. "She couldn't," he said. He shook his head and resumed pacing. "I don't think so...." His voice trailed off.

If Layla didn't see any other way out, would she have committed the murder?

Fiona moved over to the drink supply station and began preparing the beverages for our next group of guests. I joined her and said, "I think for now we need to keep focused on our task of feeding every-one." I filled a bowl with ice and placed several glasses and garnish on a tray. Fiona mixed up two more pitchers of the cocktail. "Brody, if you're going stir crazy, why don't you come with us?"

He went to the corner of the kitchen and retrieved his camera bag. That must've felt like a security blanket for him. I couldn't imagine him without it in his hands for very long. I looked at Fiona. "It's probably OK," she said.

I was sure Barney would inform us if there was an issue. I wasn't sure taking any more pictures was a good idea, but maybe his eye could catch something that could be a clue. The list of suspects was growing by the minute. Having Brody tag along with us might provide some insight into his behavior when we got to the bridal suite. At least this way we could keep tabs on him.

CHAPTER SEVEN

"Where's the chef?" Barney inquired, scanning the kitchen as if he expected to find him hiding behind the counter.

"He's delivering the food to the group upstairs," Linda said.

Barney entered the room, looking in all corners. I guess there could be clues, but for the life of me, I couldn't see what he was searching for. From the opposite end of the room, he turned and rubbed his chin, pondering something unseen by my eyes.

"OK. Well, that's good," Barney said, distracted. He picked up a few pans of bread and peered underneath. "That will keep folks busy."

Fiona brought the tray of cocktail pitchers into the kitchen and set it on the counter. "We're just about to head outside with the groom's family. We're starting everyone off with drinks," she said.

Barney stepped next to Fiona. "I guess that's alright. Save me one. I think I'm going to need it when this is over. You were right about the drama, Tilly," he said.

"What do you mean?" I asked.

"It was almost impossible for the crime scene techs to do their job. Layla wouldn't leave Aiden's side." Barney picked up a piece of yellow bell pepper and tossed it into his mouth. "Totally understandable, but it seems like she was being overly dramatic." He grabbed a slice of bread and began snacking. I only hoped Chef Ricardo wasn't counting on that to be part of his meals. That would completely set him off again, after Linda's expert touch had calmed him down.

"Yeah, it probably becomes second nature to them after a while, unnoticeable when they're acting," I said.

Brody had strapped his camera around his neck, ready for photos at a moment's notice. "You know, it could be that she is just really upset. I mean, this isn't normal, even for actors." He fiddled with the lens cap, snapping it on and off.

Barney glanced at me. "I'm sorry, Brody. I didn't realize you were close to Aiden," he said.

Brody scoffed and went to retrieve a piece of bell pepper of his own. "Not him. He was never good enough for Layla. She's better off without him," he said.

Barney stepped forward, looking back at me again. I raised my eyebrows and slightly shrugged. I had no clue whether Brody was involved or not. His infatuation with Layla was more than casual. Was it possible they were even having an affair?

"Rest assured, big guy. We will solve this. One of the people in this house is a murderer. Perhaps more were involved. People always crack. It's just a matter of applying pressure at the right time in the right way." Barney pulled out his phone to respond to the buzz. He squinted at the screen and looked up. "I better get upstairs. Deputy Stevens says that with everyone sitting down to eat, they're ripe for the pickin'," he said, reaching for another slice of bell pepper. "This is good." Barney held up the vegetable, popped it into his mouth, and exited.

"We should head out," Fiona said, "and keep the assembly line going." She looked at me. "Maybe we'll discover something on our travels."

"Linda, are you OK continuing to hold the fort down in the kitchen?" I asked. I loaded my tray up for our next stop.

"Of course, dear. It seems I'm best suited to keep the peace in the kitchen. Barney might just have to hire us for his next investigation," she said.

I didn't know how I got so lucky to find her. I only hoped she would stick around after this first disastrous catering gig. She seemed to have such a relaxed, focus-on-the-positive attitude and ease about her that I could use more of myself. And then there was my wishful thinking for a romantic relationship between her and Uncle Jack.

"And Brody, have faith that the police will get to the bottom of this," Linda added.

"Huh? Oh, yeah," Brody said. He stepped to the side and snapped several pictures of the kitchen. I had never seen pictures like that as part of a wedding album. But this was no ordinary wedding ceremony.

"Let's go," Fiona said and led us from the kitchen. Keeping everyone busy, especially Brody, was a full-time job. Thankfully I had my friend to help. If she hadn't been here, I might have crumbled under the circumstances. The pressure to perform for a celebrity, let alone do well in general for my business, was a lot to own.

Brody and I followed Fiona's orders as we headed to the outside deck. Next up was the groom's family. Would we find the opposite perspective that we had heard from the bride's family? What did they think of Layla?

We meandered down the hallway, the only sound the rattling of ice cubes in the bowl. Through the sliding glass doors, I could see several of Aiden's family members standing around, talking animatedly. I was pretty sure some of them were missing. Barney would not be happy that people disobeyed his orders. Maybe I could get them back before he arrived.

Fiona opened the door and we filed out. "Hello all. We've got some beverages for you." She placed her tray on a table. I sat mine next to it. "After we start with this, the chef will be along with food."

"I should hope so," a woman said and approached the table. She helped herself to the ice and drink.

"I'm very sorry for your loss," I said. "Let me help you." I reached for the pitcher to pour.

She shoved my hand away. "I've got it. I need to do something to keep busy," she said.

Fiona stepped forward. "You must be Aiden's mother."

The woman collapsed into a chair and bowed her head, the drink firmly grasped in both hands on her lap. She nodded. Others on the deck migrated toward us, lining up to get their beverages. I inventoried in my head how much supply we had back in the kitchen in case we needed to serve everyone another round.

"He was my baby," the woman blubbered.

I busied myself with serving, anticipating silence might keep her talking.

Brody ambled off toward the railing of the deck, clicking repeatedly for more pictures. This time, the subject was the beauty of the beach.

"I told you things wouldn't end well for Aiden, Millie," a man said, standing next to the seated woman.

"Everyone has their problems," she sniped. "Look at us." She brought the drink up and sipped, keeping her focus on the gleaming liquid.

"Really? You're going to throw that in my face when our son is lying dead inside?" The man flung his arm toward the door. He grabbed the glass from me and stomped to the other side of the deck.

Millie looked up, tears streaming down her face. "No matter what, he was my son." She bowed her head. Fiona handed her a napkin. "Nobody deserves this," she blubbered.

I made eye contact with Fiona and flicked my head toward the water. I needed a break from the theater to clear my head. I figured we had a bit of time before we needed to move on to the next set of guests.

CHAPTER EIGHT

I grabbed Fiona's hand and we descended the staircase to the sand. I sat on the bottom step and removed my socks and shoes. Nothing was better than connecting directly with the earth to ground me in reality. The sun from the day had warmed the sand and it felt like a blanket on my feet. Fiona did the same and we headed north. Looking up to my right, I saw majestic homes towering over the beach. Literally, million dollar views. Each home had a wall of windows overlooking the beach. I wondered if Barney would have answers by the end of the day.

The light breeze blew my hair in a swirl, cooling my face. "Fiona, I'm more confused than ever," I said. "The more people we hear from, the farther from the truth it feels like we are."

Brody was about several hundred yards in front of us, deeply engrossed in his nature photography. Beyond Brody, a few of the groom's family were heading back toward us. I wondered what the neighbors must have thought. Several people from the wedding party wandered the beach.

"I couldn't agree more. I'm sorry I roped you into this," Fiona said. We continued our roaming.

"There was no way you could have known. Plus, truthfully? I had stars in my eyes, thinking about rubbing elbows with the rich and famous," I said. "If there's a next time, please talk me out of it."

Fiona picked up a small piece of driftwood and threw it toward the water. We moved from the soft to the hard, wet sand, easing our walk. All I needed was a pulled muscle. We wound our way through sporadic pieces of seaweed deposited by the waves. I turned over my shoulder to see how far we had come from the house. Looking at my watch, I estimated we had only been gone about five minutes.

"Do you have any thoughts?" Fiona asked. Her long blond hair fluttered in the wind, her swing dress ruffling around her knees.

I laughed. "Lots of them. None very organized." I turned back toward the direction we had come from, feeling a need to get back to the job.

"I doubt that. You're the queen of organization," Fiona said.

"Yeah. I do like to have things in order. But this is one of those times that I feel like you pull a thread and get a sweater," I said. The obvious was nothing close to what it appeared to be. And the innocuous could be the answer to the mystery. "Let's start close. How about Brody?"

Fiona stopped and looked at me. "That's a tough one. As far as Layla? He's head over heels. So how far would he go to protect her? Aiden? Had he seen enough of his deplorable behavior that it was the last straw?"

"Maybe," I responded. "We definitely can't rule him out. And he was nearby when we heard the scream. But as the wedding photographer, you would expect him to be everywhere." I kicked the sand. "Ugh. OK. He stays on the list."

"What if he and Layla were in on it together? Maybe they planned it all along," Fiona said.

Yes, we had yet to hear from the bride, other than her dramatic scene after discovering the body. On our next stop at the bridal suite I would pay extra attention to Brody and Layla's interactions. That had to provide clues one way or another.

"Let's move on. What about the bride's family?" I asked.

"We really need to get a notebook like Deputy Stevens has. When I see things written down, I'm better able to connect the dots," Fiona said.

I couldn't agree more. As I visualized the suspects and clues in this case, the picture became infinitely more complicated. Truth was most definitely stranger than fiction. You just couldn't make this stuff up.

We had returned almost half the distance to the house and had no more clarity than when we started our walk. If possible, the picture was even more muddled. I had never seen so many people that wanted someone out of the way, each with their own unique reason.

"Layla's father jumps to the top of my list," I said. "The vitriol in his voice when he spoke of Aiden—he almost spit when he was talking about how he treated Layla." The towering figure of Layla's father could have overpowered Aiden. Were they having an argument that got out of hand? Though I might not understand it, I had heard that protective gene would make parents stop at nothing to take care of their children. That motive was as strong as any other. If her father hadn't been able to reason with Layla up until the end, did he attempt another means to stop the wedding?

"I agree. There was just something about that man that scared me a little bit too," Fiona said. She was one of the most courageous people I knew. For him to frighten her said something.

We had reached the bottom of the staircase. I sat again and brushed sand from my feet. Brody and the rest of the groom's crew were returning to the house. A loud whistle came from up above. I looked up and saw Barney standing at the edge of the deck, waving everyone his direction. Behind him, the chef's team was diligently preparing to serve the food.

I glanced at Fiona. Our analysis was far from over. The groom's family appeared to be off the hook. Why would they kill one of their own? If anyone, Layla might be their target. Or Brody, if he had portrayed Aiden in a poor light. I gulped. Thankfully, Barney had the foresight to separate the groups or we might have more bloodshed. And how had Aiden actually died? With a killer on the loose, maybe they weren't done.

"Fiona," I whispered as we slowly made our way to the deck. "What if the killer isn't done?"

She grabbed both of my arms, staring into my eyes. "You're right!"

"I need everyone up here," Barney ordered.

I turned to look at Brody and the remainder of the groom's family as we complied with the instruction. Standing at the edge of the deck, I scanned the crowd, pondering each face as I wondered if any of them were involved.

"Ladies." Barney approached us. "This system is working very well. Go ahead on to the bridal party and get them started with cocktails." The sides of his mouth slightly raised and he leaned in. "Might have to contract with the both of you for future investigation work." He turned and began his process with the groom's family.

I stepped over to Brody, his eyes glazed over. "C'mon, Brody," I said.

He blinked, staring off toward the neighboring house. I gently touched his elbow and guided him to the door. I really hoped he wasn't involved in the murder. And that Layla hadn't conned him into doing something for her. He seemed to have a genuine concern and I wanted to believe he was innocent, just getting caught up in the glitz like most everyone else who came into contact with a celebrity.

Fiona, Brody, and I stepped inside to a momentary peace.

CHAPTER NINE

The sounds from the deck joined the murmurs and sniffles we heard behind the door of the bridal suite. This might be the moment of truth when we visited Layla and her bridesmaids. First, we needed to replenish our supplies before we hit the road again. Fiona reached behind her and tugged Brody's arm. He obediently followed.

"Fiona, I hope you brought enough stock to hold us for a while," I said. "And for you and me when this is all over." I escorted our little merry band of beverage deliveries down the hallway to the kitchen. Without missing much of a beat, the chef sounded like he had returned to his previous antics. Pots and pans clanged, and his voice grumbled to reflect his unhappy mood. "And maybe more for chef too."

I turned the corner to see the chef holding a yellow bell pepper in each hand. "Who has been sneaking my supplies?" He shook a vegetable around the room in all directions. "I plan meticulously to have just what I need. Waste not, want not. And to discover we also have a thief on our hands in addition to a murder!"

We all stepped back, unsure if a pepper might just be coming at our heads. More likely something inedible, but nonetheless we wanted to avoid any projectiles.

"Chef Ricardo," Linda interjected. "I understand you're upset. But everyone here is under a lot of stress. And we're all doing the best we can under very trying circumstances." She removed the peppers from his hands and placed them near the cutting boards, also angling him away from the knives. *Smooth move, Linda.*

"You're right, Miss Linda. I'm sorry," he said and bowed his head. "I just wanted this to be my best event yet. And..." his voice drifted away. Linda guided him to a side table where he compliantly sat in the chair she proffered.

"We all do," Linda said. She gestured to Fiona to prepare another cocktail for the chef. If my brain was in gear at all I would have served the chef before anyone else. We needed him to be fully engaged.

Fiona quickly prepared the drink and delivered it to the chef. He tipped his head up. I chose to believe the expression on his face was a smile and not a smirk. Fiona began making two more pitchers of cocktails for our next stop at the bridal suite.

"Miss Linda?" Chef Ricardo asked. He reached out his hand toward her.

"Yes, Chef?" she said and leaned in.

Chef Ricardo scanned the room, returning his gaze to Linda. We were all raptly watching this scene. Was he smitten with her? She had certainly charmed him with her pleasant personality. Was he going to hit on her in the midst of this turmoil, with a job to do? Quietly, he said, "When this is all over, would you come to work with me?"

Linda's glance darted my direction. He was trying to steal my assistant just as we were getting started. That little scoundrel. *I guess nothing ventured, nothing gained.* "Umm." I stepped forward.

Linda slightly turned her body toward the chef. "While that's a lovely offer, I am working for Tilly."

The chef stood and drained his drink. "Well," he said, looking at me. "If it doesn't work out..." He turned and strode back to the head of the counter, apparently ready to bark out orders again to his crew.

Fiona held her fist to her mouth, covering a snicker. It would be entertaining in a way if it wasn't under such tragic conditions.

We had gotten our system down, filling supplies and delivering drinks. My only hope was by the time we reached our final destination that Barney had enough information to make an arrest.

"Brody," I said. "Let's head to the bridal suite."

His head popped up and he stood at attention. Any opportunity to see Layla. From this point on I needed to be on high alert. I stepped to Fiona's side, my back to Brody as I lifted the tray. "Let's keep a really close eye on Brody and Layla's interactions," I said.

"Agreed," Fiona replied.

Linda had moved on to the next round of plating for the cheesecakes. By all indications from the guests, they were thrilled with the food and the dessert. "Linda, can I do anything to help?" I asked.

She lined up plates and had begun slicing the next cheesecake from the refrigerator. The tiramisu cheesecake was one of the best-tasting options we had provided the couple. It was my personal favorite also because of the ease of preparation. It looked like you had spent days on the dessert. The chef peeked his head up, observing us. I acknowledged him and he returned to his task.

Linda said, "Nope. Totally under control." She placed each slice on a plate, topped with a dollop of cream and a sprinkle of cocoa powder. My stomach growled, reminding me I hadn't eaten a thing since breakfast. My plan to take a break after getting the cheesecakes into the cooler was completely out the window. And there would be no snacking on the chef's food. At least not without his permission.

Fiona and I loaded up and headed out, with Brody tagging along like a little brother. On our way to the bridal suite, we passed by the room where the crime scene techs were finishing up and packing their tools. I glanced into the room as we went by, willing my mind to see something that would be a clue to solving this whole mess. Almost nothing looked out of place with Aiden. His professionally coifed blond curls. His navy tux with the lily boutonniere. His shiny black shoes.

One of the techs raised their head. "We're just finishing up," she said. There was nothing in her voice that let on what they had discovered. I suspected they would meet with Barney before they left. If there were any way possible, I had to eavesdrop on that conversation.

I hurried by the room, my heart racing. "Fiona," I said.

She stopped just before entering the bridal suite, her brows furrowed. "What is it? Did you see something?" Her gaze darted between me and the direction of Aiden's body.

I shook my head. "No. I just realized. Do you think we're considered suspects?" I gulped. Why wouldn't we be? Everyone here was likely under suspicion until they weren't. Barney couldn't afford to play favorites just because he knew us. This epiphany shed a whole new light. One that provided a really ugly picture. In this small town, how did Barney stay neutral in these cases, knowing possibly someone he knew could be responsible for something so heinous? My immense respect for him just shot through the roof. I didn't know that I could ever be unemotional enough to do what he does.

"Tilly, I think Barney will do his job. And quickly we'll be off the list." Fiona looked at Brody. Well, some of us might remain on until further notice. I hoped with all my heart that sweet guy had nothing to do with this. Into the lioness's den we headed.

CHAPTER TEN

y mind reeled with possibilities, including Fiona and myself as suspects. My clammy hands shook as I held the tray. With no doubt Fiona and I were innocent, why was I still so nervous?

Fiona looked at me. "Tilly, everything will work out the way it's supposed to. Have faith." She tapped on the door and reached for the handle.

Looking back at Brody's drawn face, my heart was heavy. He stood on his tiptoes to see past Fiona into the room. We filed in to see all of the bridesmaids seated in a semi-circle around Layla. In unison, they lifted their heads our direction.

"Oh, Layla," Brody whined, rushing around us. He held out his arms. Layla looked at her entourage as if questioning what her response should be. How tiring it must be to live in the spotlight and always feel like you have to calculate every move for your image.

Layla stood and Brody enveloped her in his arms. His eyes closed. Layla pushed back, dabbing her nose and eyes with a tissue. "I can't believe he's gone," she blubbered and plopped back into the chair. She straightened out the lower portion of her dress like she was preparing for a photo shoot.

Brody took her hand and crouched next to her chair. "I'm here for you. No matter what," he said.

"So are we," the bridesmaids chimed in.

Emma stepped forward. "Layla, just trust that you will come out of this better than before." She bent to hug her and grabbed Layla's other hand.

Fiona and I made eye contact and moved to a table on the side of the room. We set the trays down and began preparing the beverages. Fiona grabbed her throat and stuck her tongue out. I nodded. It was getting pretty deep in here. We had seen the beginning of what we suspected as Brody continued to fawn over Layla. Was he just starstruck? Or was there a genuine caring for her?

Pouring two glasses, Fiona grabbed them and started passing out the beverages to the ladies. "We thought you could use a drink," she said.

I took two glasses and handed one to Emma, one to Layla. "The chef will be here soon with some food. You should eat something. We don't know how long we'll be here," I said.

Layla stood. "Brody, I can't stay here any longer." Her eyes pleaded with him. "Do something!"

"My love," Brody started and slyly looked around the room. "I think we have to wait until we're interviewed."

"I can't take it anymore," Layla said and shoved Brody aside. "My husb—" She bowed her head. "I mean, my fiancé, is lying in the room next door and I'm just supposed to sit here compliant and take it?" Layla yelled.

Now was about the time I wished Linda had joined us on our travels. She was kind of like a therapy dog, easing people's anxiety. Was Layla about to bolt from the room? What was our obligation to detain her? I guess I could run up and get Barney or the deputy if that happened. Didn't we already have enough drama?

"I agree with Emma. And if you admit to yourself, finally, you have to concur that you are better off without Aiden," Brody said.

It felt like the oxygen in the room had evaporated. It was one thing to think that. It was another to say it behind her back. But Brody had laid it all out right in front of Layla.

Layla turned toward Emma. "You pretend to be my friend. You're just jealous that Aiden chose me and not you!" She pointed her finger in Emma's face.

If I hadn't seen it with my own eyes, I wasn't sure I would have believed it. They were turning on each other. I closed my eyes, making mental notes of the interactions to share later with Barney. There had to be some juicy clues in that exchange between the bride and maid of honor. What was the history with Emma and Layla? And was there history between Emma and Aiden?

I nudged Fiona and flicked my head toward the cocktails. If one round would loosen their lips this much, should we dare go for a second? We met at the side table. "Let's see how far they go. Then we can offer round two, if needed," I whispered.

Fiona nodded and we stood back, watching the show. Thankfully she was here to witness it all with me.

Emma shoved Layla back into the chair. "Get your finger out of my face. We're all stressed out, not just you."

Brody stood and inserted himself between the two women. "Hey," he said, looking between them like he was a referee at a prize fight.

"You've always been jealous of me. Everything I get, you want as your own. Even if it's not right for you," Layla said. She stood and began pacing the small space in the room, her long train whooshing as she made the turns.

Emma approached her. "That's not true. We've always been in this together. From the time we were little and cast in that movie, *Bad Egg*."

Layla's mouth tried for a smile. "That was fun," she said.

Emma took Layla's hand and returned her to the chair, handing her another drink. "And I wasn't jealous one bit that you got the lead and I didn't," she said. "It's always been the two of us against the world."

"Brody?" Layla asked softly. "You've always been there for me. Could you find out when we can leave?" She batted her imitation eyelashes at him. I was pretty sure there wasn't much he wouldn't do for her.

Brody turned and headed toward the door. Fiona stepped in front of him and shook her head.

"C'mon. We've been patient enough. This has to end," Brody said. He pulled his shoulders back and puffed out his chest. Now he was putting on a show for the room. As if willing it, the door opened.

Chef Ricardo bounded in, heading straight for Layla. With out-stretched arms, he said, "Oh, my dear. I am so sorry." He wrapped her in a hug. "I only hope my cuisine will bring you even the tiniest of comfort." That was quite the turnaround from the guy who called the bride a brat earlier. He turned and swept him arm toward the door. "We have a feast fit for a queen," he said, waving his staff in. One by one they delivered the plates of food to the bridal party.

"You always know how to treat a girl right," Layla said.

This crew was ripe for the picking. I only hoped Barney would be along soon to see some of what had developed. I couldn't tell exactly how, but my gut said we were getting closer to having answers. I supposed if you sequestered people long enough, they started to crack and turn on each other. Fiona and I stood back, soaking it all in. Brody had his arm around Layla, and she let him soothe her. I had no doubt that in time he would see her true colors and his heart would be shattered. There was no way to avoid that disaster.

CHAPTER ELEVEN

I closed the door behind us as we exited the bridal suite. For now, there was no way to separate Brody and Layla. Barney would just have to deal with it. I exhaled loudly. "Oh, Fiona. This is getting complicated."

We headed to the kitchen for our final trip to the groom's suite, sans Brody. "I guess. You want to believe celebrities are just normal people," Fiona said. She gestured over her shoulder. "But I don't know what to think anymore," Fiona said. "The list of suspects is long."

"You got that right. Just give me Unkie and my little bakery, and I'm a happy camper," I said.

We turned into the kitchen. Thankfully, Chef Ricardo and his team were out on deliveries. I needed some quiet to clear my head. A pain behind my right eye had developed that I was sure wouldn't leave until we could put this wedding in the rearview mirror.

"What happened?" Linda asked, her eyebrows furrowed. She pulled out two chairs at the counter for Fiona and me to sit. I wasn't sure we had much time, but I needed a short rest. "You look like you've been through the ringer."

"This is exhausting. I can't imagine what I would do without you here," I said, looking at Fiona. "It feels like it's not going to end."

Fiona reached out her hand. "We just have to keep doing our part so Barney can do his," she said.

I slipped off the chair and straightened my apron. "I know. We're almost done. This was just far from the vision I had for this event." I shook out my arms, the tension easing a bit.

"Maybe a report from home will perk you up a bit. Think about what you have to look forward to," Linda said. I was blessed to be surrounding myself with incredibly positive and supportive people. I couldn't ask for anything more.

I reached over and gave Linda a squeeze. "Oooohh. Tell me."

I clapped my hands. Ever since I had adopted my little kitten, my life had been even more of an adventure. My little Peanut was a huge snuggler. When I held her close, she looked up at me with appreciation in her eyes. She was also incredibly playful. We had gotten into a routine after I got home from work where we would play hide-and-seek. With no experience owning a pet, I had no idea what to expect. When I came through the door, I would call out for her. She would let out a little peep. Every day would be a different spot. As soon as I found her, she would run and jump into my arms. I would hold her tight, closing my eyes, grateful for the moment.

Linda laughed. "Truthfully, I think Jack is having a ball. But he said never again would he be the kitty daycare."

"You really get him," I said to Linda. Their banter made it appear as if they had known each other for decades.

Linda turned away and fidgeted with her earring. "I guess I do," she said.

Fiona looked at me, eyes wide. I nodded. If a girl could hope, I wished a romantic relationship for Linda and Unkie. I wouldn't push. Everything in time. I just wondered how long it would be before they admitted to what we could all see clear as day.

Talk of the kittens, and thinking about more than this calamity, had eased the tension in my shoulders. I rolled them around a few times, preparing for our last delivery to the groomsmen.

Giving me an elbow jab, Fiona passed by me and headed to prepare the final servings. I eyeballed the supplies to see if there would be leftovers for us. I could use one or two of Fiona's signature cocktails about now. This would be a story for the ages.

"Hey there." Barney poked his head into the kitchen.

We all jumped, Fiona sloshing liquid over the side of the pitcher in her hand.

"Sorry about that. I guess everyone is on pins and needles. Where's Brody?" Barney asked, scanning the kitchen.

I stepped forward, hoping I wasn't about to get admonished for leaving him with Layla. "He's in the bridal suite. We couldn't tear him away," I said.

Barney shook his head. "Seriously, when passion comes into the picture, why do people lose their minds? It certainly keeps me in business."

"Oops. Should we go get him?" I asked.

"Nah. I'm headed there now. It's fine," Barney replied. "If you all can hang in there just a bit longer, we're almost done. And"—Barney pointed at Linda—"I understand I have you to thank for keeping the chef under control. There might just be a commendation coming for that."

He was right. It had been quite the team effort to pull this off. I stared at Barney, trying to glean from his expression whether he had made progress on identifying the killer. He looked my direction and, as if reading my mind, said, "Not yet, Tilly. But every piece fills out the puzzle picture just a bit more. I'm optimistic before we leave that I'll have what I need."

I shivered. Somewhere in our midst, we were face-to-face with a killer. I rattled the names and faces through the Rolodex in my brain. Lots of possibilities, but no obvious culprits yet, at least to me.

Fiona laughed. "He nailed you." She finished packing up the supplies for our trip to the groomsmen's suite. We followed Barney out of the kitchen. He turned toward the bride's room and we headed to see the guys.

Whispering to Fiona, I said, "Do you think any of the guys are part of this?"

"Not sure," she replied. "Let's do the same thing when we go in there as we did with the bridesmaids. Observe their reactions to everything." She tapped on the door and entered.

All five guys stood as we entered, at least putting on the appearance of behaving like gentleman. The best man, Cooper, reached for Fiona's tray and set it on a side table. He returned for mine and placed it next to Fiona's.

"Hey, there," Fiona started. "I'm sorry it's taken us so long to get to you."

Cooper stepped forward. "What's happening? Nobody will tell us a thing. And we're stuck in here, our minds running wild with possibilities." He resumed his seat.

Fiona began preparing drinks, so I decided to answer his question. Looking at each one of the guys, I couldn't see anything obvious in their mannerisms or expressions that looked suspicious. Their faces were grim, like you might expect in a situation like this. Except it was anything but normal.

"The chief said it shouldn't be much longer. Plus, the chef will be here soon with some food," I said. Fiona handed me drinks as she finished preparing each one. I took one and handed it to Cooper. He hung his head, looking like he might lose it. He looked up with tears in his eyes. I spotted a box of tissues on a side table and snagged a handful, offering them to Cooper.

CHAPTER TWELVE

"Cooper, get over it," one of the guys said and began pacing the room.

I handed him a drink to keep him occupied—and hopefully to settle him down. That's all we needed was an unruly group for our last delivery of the day.

"Shut up, Dave." Cooper sniffled, wiping his nose with the wad and throwing them into the small trashcan next to his chair. "I'm not broken over Aiden. We all know he wasn't good for Layla. Just nobody had the guts to say it before now or do anything about it."

The other guy continued pacing and sipping his drink. Fiona handed me another beverage to pass along. I continued serving the guys until each had a glass in their hands. I joined Fiona on the side of the room to further observe the interactions between the groomsmen.

Dave stopped his pacing and stood in front of Cooper. "You didn't do something, did you?" He gazed at the others in the room to gauge their reactions to his question and returned his focus toward Cooper.

Cooper shook his head and remained silent. Was he denying involvement or keeping quiet, holding in his guilt?

"C'mon, man," another one of the guys said, moving to join Dave in front of Cooper. "If you were involved in this, they will find out."

Were we about to witness a confession? Now would be the perfect time to have that little notebook and pen to capture everything that was going down. Thankfully, Fiona was here for a second set of eyes and ears to help relay anything critical to Barney. We stood like statues, hoping this continued to play out further in our presence.

Standing, Cooper was inches from the two guys confronting him. "I said," he spat through gritted teeth, "I didn't have anything to do with this. Maybe it was one of you." He stepped away and pointed to each of the guys in the room. Was that just a diversion tactic? If I didn't know any better, he seemed genuinely upset. Although, not so much for the groom.

The drinks weren't having the desired effect on this group. "We should all take a breath. This is stressful for everyone," I said, hoping to quell the tension.

Dave took a seat, sitting back and slowly crossing his legs. He picked an imaginary piece of lint from his pants. "Dude, we all know you had the hots for Layla," he said.

A couple of the guys mumbled their concurrence with Dave's revelation. Cooper approached Fiona with his empty glass, requesting a refill. She grabbed the pitcher and filled it up, making the rounds to top off the drinks of the others as well.

Did Cooper know how bad Aiden treated Layla? Would he have stepped in at the last second, desperate to stop the wedding to keep them apart? He was the best man. He must have known all along about their tumultuous relationship.

Cooper turned to face the room. "He didn't deserve her. I tried talking to him so many times about how he treated her. It just seemed to embolden him further, like he felt he was untouchable."

"Sorry, dude," Dave said. "I'm not accusing you. But who could it be? Someone in this house is a killer."

I wasn't letting Cooper off the hook. No matter how upset he was, his emotions may have gotten the best of him in a last-ditch effort to save Layla. I scanned the room and closed my eyes, imprinting the details in my brain. I opened my eyes and touched Fiona's arm, gesturing toward the door. Likely the chef would arrive soon with the food. We probably had all of the evidence we might get for now from this group.

We left the room and closed the door behind us. I took a deep breath, feeling the exhaustion settling into my muscles. "What do you think?" I whispered to Fiona.

She held her palms up and shrugged. "It's a long list. Most of the motives center around Aiden's poor treatment of Layla. But who is the one that took their actions too far? And how did they do it? Especially with so many people around."

"I know. The more people we talk to, the more convoluted it gets. I feel like there's just one thing that will break this wide open. But what is it?" I asked. We started our trek to the kitchen. We might as well start cleaning up. Hopefully we could be released soon to go home. My mind drifted to thoughts of my little furry Peanut and that made me smile.

We silently strolled along the hallway, passing the room with Aiden. With the techs gone, the coroner would soon remove the body. I stopped in the doorway, hoping one last time for a clue to materialize before me. I forced my eyes and brain to focus, slowly scanning the room from left to right, then Aiden's body from top to bottom. His clothes were identical to the groomsmen, except his vest was a different color.

I grabbed Fiona's arm. "We have to find Brody and look at his pictures again," I said.

"Tilly, what is it?" she asked.

We left Aiden and moved along to the bridal suite, sure we would find Brody still there. Listening through the door, we heard a low rumble of conversation. I gulped and lightly tapped the door so I didn't startle anyone more than they already were on edge.

"Hi all," I said, entering the room. "We came for the empty dishes. We're starting to clean up." The women had drained the pitcher of cocktails and had nibbled on the food from the chef. I hoped Chef Ricardo didn't see how much was left over, otherwise he might lose it. Everyone continued to surround Layla like she was leading them in story time. If I could only have been a fly on the wall to hear what tale she was telling.

Fiona started piling everything onto the trays, the only sound dishes clanking together.

I turned toward the group. "Brody?" I said.

He slowly lifted his head, his eyes glazed over like he was in a trance. "Huh?" he asked.

"Can you come with us back to the kitchen?" I asked. I stepped over to him and held out my hand. He took it and hoisted himself up, looking back at Layla. I slightly tugged to get his attention.

"Will you be OK?" he asked Layla.

"I don't know how I'll ever be OK again. I've lost the love of my life," she answered, burying her head in her hands.

I wasn't buying it. Her antics looked more like a child who was just making noise as opposed to real tears of sorrow.

I pointed toward the corner of the room. "Don't forget your camera," I said to Brody.

He zombie-walked to retrieve his bag and followed Fiona and me from the room. That was almost too easy. We led him back to the kitchen where I hoped to get a peek at his photos again. It was probably nothing, but I had to see it with my own eyes to be sure. If the picture didn't provide any clarity, I was at a loss. I only hoped Barney's expertise could put the pieces together.

CHAPTER THIRTEEN

Linda had kept herself busy cleaning the entire kitchen while the rest of us had been out and about. It was spotless. That was well above and beyond what we had been hired for. If she was anything like me, she needed to keep busy to feel productive. She acknowledged the three of us as we entered, taking Fiona's tray. Looking at Brody, she asked, "Are you OK?"

He nodded, appearing to remain under Layla's spell. She hadn't given him the time of day, except to lean on him about her loss. It didn't seem she even had a clue about how he felt about her.

Brody hoisted his camera bag onto the counter and plopped into a chair, his arms limp at his sides. No answer to Linda's question.

Linda stepped forward and put her arm around his shoulder and squeezed. "Barney will figure this out. And we'll all be on our way soon," she said. Her confidence boosted my spirits. I was hopeful but not optimistic. With an endless number of suspects, solving this mystery might take quite a bit of time, unless someone cracked under the pressure.

I stepped to the counter and asked Brody, "Would you mind if I take a look?"

He swiveled his head my direction and closed his eyes. I took that as assent and unzipped the camera bag. Brody reached over and turned on the camera and the screen came to life.

"Push this button to scroll through," he said and turned away.

I moved over to Fiona so we could scan the pictures together. I had a few specific shots I wanted to see. My stomach rumbled, making me feel like I was on the edge of a breakthrough more than it reminded me I hadn't eaten. My hands began to clam up. I wiped each one on my apron. I began looping through the photos in reverse order that they had been taken. I stopped at one of the last photos of Aiden alive and pointed. Fiona's hand slapped over her mouth. I continued back through to near the beginning to find what I was looking for. An early photo of Aiden popped up, and I pointed again. Fiona's eyes bulged and she nodded.

It was something, but it might not mean a thing. I had to find Barney and share my discovery. "Will you be OK here with them?" I asked Fiona.

"Yes, go." She looked at Linda and Brody, still huddled at the counter. "We'll be fine."

Heading out of the kitchen, I stopped for a second, calculating where Barney would be in his investigation. The chef had already been to the bridal suite, so possibly Barney was there. If not that, the groomsmen. I headed down the hallway, more certain than ever that my discovery would be enlightening. If it wasn't the final clue, hopefully it at least clarified the direction questioning should take and who should be on the hot seat.

I whizzed by the room with Aiden and speed walked to the room with the bride. I barged in, not interested in tiptoeing around anyone's feelings anymore. No matter what Aiden was guilty of, he didn't deserve to be murdered. I scanned, and not seeing Barney, exited to head to the groomsmen's suite. My heart raced with the urgency of finding Barney to share my theory and expose the killer before he let everyone go.

Stopping just outside the groomsmen's room I breathed in deeply. I needed my wits and to be able to speak clearly when I had the opportunity. Barney was inside, interviewing the final group. I hesitated, not wanting to interrupt his flow. I paced outside the door, looking at my watch. I stopped in my tracks. Did I get it wrong? The pictures left no doubt, but maybe there was a reasonable explanation. Sometimes truth was stranger than fiction. I would provide Barney the evidence and let him be the one to make sense of it.

The door opened and I greeted Barney as he left the room. He closed the door behind him and shook his head. I wasn't sure how to interpret that gesture, but I echoed the feeling. From the visits with each of the groups, my suspicion grew of almost everyone. I supposed if we were all put in this situation, our behavior might mirror what I had seen over the last several hours. The fact that many of the guests were actors only amped up the drama.

I looked around to ensure nobody else was in earshot. Holding out the camera, I said, "I found something." I stood to Barney's side. "There are a few pictures I want you to see. It might be absolutely nothing."

The corners of Barney's mouth slightly lifted. He would probably take whatever break he could get. This crowd was a doozy. He bowed his head over the small screen, squinting. "OK. Narrate for me what I'm seeing," he said.

I began near the end of the sequence, pointing to one where Aiden was on the floor. I tipped the screen in Barney's direction. He nodded.

I moved through most of the pictures until I got to the set Brody had taken earlier in the day. Two specific pictures told a story. I only hoped Barney could nail the plot and characters to this story. I tapped the screen to enlarge the next photo, pointing to the item of interest. Barney looked at me, eyes widened. That gesture confirmed I may have been on the right track. I moved to the final picture and held it for him to see.

"Tilly, I think you've done it," Barney said. "May I?" He reached for the camera, moving back and forth between the last two pictures, shaking his head. "This is the last piece to the puzzle. I've narrowed down my list of suspects to three. But this seals the deal." Barney strapped the camera over his shoulder. I hoped Brody wouldn't be upset that his prized possession might be confiscated as part of the investigation. I suspected he would give it up for Layla in a heartbeat.

"What's next, Barney?" I asked. I felt we were on the downhill slide, soon to be released to go home.

He rubbed his chin and said, "Tell you what. Can you assemble everyone in the room where the ceremony had been planned to occur?"

I nodded. "Sure. It'll take a few minutes. But I'm sure we can do it quickly because I think people want out of here as much as they want answers."

Barney looked at the pictures again, holding out the camera. "This is gold." He pulled out his notebook and jotted a few things down. "I'll go find Deputy Stevens and meet everyone back here ASAP."

I decided to go to the room farthest away first. The bride's family upstairs would be the first released to join the gathering. I quickly huffed up the stairs, glad my running was finally paying off. One by one I visited the groom's family outside, the bridal suite, and the groomsmen, directing them to the great room. Each group quizzed me for information about what was happening. I had an inkling, but it wasn't my role to reveal. My last stop was the kitchen to let everyone know we were in the home stretch.

CHAPTER FOURTEEN

I raced back to the great room, standing to the side to watch everyone enter and take their seats. Layla and Emma had linked arms, and Layla was loudly whimpering, much more than she had when I last visited the bridal suite. They proceeded to the front left of the room and took their seats. In turn, the bridesmaids and bride's friends and family chose seats behind them, and the groom's friends and family took the opposite section.

Stepping in behind everyone, the kitchen crew entered and took up a place standing behind the guests. If this story didn't warrant a big motion picture movie, I didn't know what did.

Barney and Deputy Stevens stood at the front of the room as if they were going to officiate a wedding. Chef Ricardo proceeded down the aisle toward Barney, turned, and faced the crowd. "I want to thank you for hiring me to cater—"

Stepping forward, Barney touched the chef's arm. "Chef," he whispered.

Chef Ricardo turned and raised his arms in the air. He rattled off some unpleasant words in Italian and stomped back down the aisle, joining his team at the back of the room. "Far be it from me to try and get a good review from a bad situation," he said under his breath, but loud enough for everyone to hear.

"Ladies and gentlemen. First, let me thank you for your patience under very difficult circumstances," Barney started.

From the left side of the room, the bride's father Norman stood and pointed in the direction of the groom's family. "You should have kept Aiden away from my princess. And this never would have happened," he bellowed.

"How dare you." The groom's father stood on the other side of the room.

Barney stepped down and moved to the middle of the aisle, his arms gesturing for the two men to sit. They glared at each other, looked at Barney, and complied.

"If you can all give me your attention, we will soon be out of here," Barney said and returned to the front of the room.

Mumblings continued from both sides, but not enough to disturb his progress. Reaching into his pocket, Barney pulled out a flower and raised his arm above his head. "This, ladies and gentleman, is the key to this mystery."

Heads turned with quizzical looks as to why Barney was holding up a calla lily boutonniere. The volume of the mumbling rose.

Norman stood again and pointed at Barney. "Quit trying to slow walk us with your cutesy theatrics," he barked.

Layla's blubbering filled the room, practically echoing off the walls. "Aiden loved lilies," she screamed and collapsed against Emma.

Barney moved in front of the duo and held out the flower in front of Emma, who leaned her head against Layla's shoulder. He didn't say a word. It felt like several minutes went by before anyone spoke.

Still standing behind his daughter, Norman asked, "What's the meaning of this?" He looked around to garner support for his questioning of the police chief. "You better have a good explanation for badgering those young women, or so help me..."

Layla's mom touched Norman's arm, and he looked down at her. She patted the seat next to her and he silently dropped into it, continuing to glare at Barney. Little did Norman know, Barney had the best explanation of all.

"Why do you have Aiden's boutonniere?" Layla asked, looking up at Barney. "Why would you take that off of him?" She reached out to take the flower.

Barney remained in front of Emma, moving the flower out of Layla's reach.

"Wait a minute." Layla stood. "He still had his boutonniere on when he—" She brought her hand up to her face and resumed crying. Norman moved to the front of the room and wrapped his daughter in his arms.

"Why indeed? Emma, would you like to explain?" Barney asked.

Emma knocked the flower from his hand and stood, reaching for Layla. "Don't listen to him. Layla, Aiden wasn't good for you." Emma placed her hand on Layla's shoulder. "This was the best thing," she said.

Barney retrieved the flower and stood back. With his simple prompting, Emma's words flowed like a raging river. "What are you talking about?" Layla turned and faced Emma. "You know I loved him."

"I know that. And I couldn't see why he chose you over me. You're always so full of yourself. And your dad makes sure you get whatever you want," Emma said. Her fists were balled up like she was ready to take a swing.

Sensing that same intention, Barney stepped in. "Deputy Stevens, please take Emma into custody for the murder of Aiden," he ordered.

"If I couldn't have him, you weren't going to either," Emma spat. She wrestled her arms from the deputy, finally giving in to being handcuffed.

Layla and her dad sunk into a chair in the front row as we watched the spectacle of Emma in a ball gown trying to wriggle out of the deputy's grasp. "I finally beat you at something," she yelled as they left the room.

From the corner of my eye, I saw someone sprint to the front, joining Layla and her dad. Brody wrapped his arms around the bride. She reached up and held his hand.

"I knew she was jealous of me, always beating her out for parts. But until now, she wasn't that good of an actress," Layla said, shaking her head. "But to kill Aiden?"

As Chef Ricardo started down the aisle again, Linda grabbed his arm. "I think we're almost done," she whispered. He obediently returned to his place.

Barney returned to the front of the room, holding up the tattered flower. The muttering immediately stopped. "Thanks to Brody's photography and Tilly's eagle eye, the murderer and the weapon were identified." You could have heard a pin drop. Heads were swiveling all around to see if anyone else had a clue what Barney was referring to.

"For the love of Pete!" Norman said. A few people chuckled, releasing tension.

Barney might be able to break into the acting world after this. He was adopting a flair for the dramatic. "Allegedly, Emma altered one of the extra boutonnieres to add an exceptionally long pin. The problem was, she chose a version that the groomsmen wore, not one like the groom." Barney pointed to the flower that must have been discarded by Emma. He noted that the complementary green with the white lily had more layers for the groom's version. The camera had first shown Aiden with it on, then another picture where Emma was pinning a different flower onto his lapel.

"I'm sorry for your loss," Barney said to Layla.

She shook her head and turned into Brody's waiting arms. I didn't know what the future had in store for either of them, but if Brody had his way, Layla would be his bride. I only hoped she saw the sweet guy who deeply cared for her.

Getting back to a routine after the nightmare catering event was a welcome experience. Linda and I had developed a system where we could produce our orders in about half the time it had taken me as a solo baker. Even though we were efficient, it was blatantly clear that the small kitchen in the corner of Uncle Jack's Checkered Past Antiques shop was no longer serving the need. The kindness and generosity of Unkie to carve out a space for me was unparalleled.

Making the decision to move to my own place was bittersweet. Thankfully, we weren't moving far down the boardwalk. The owner of Poppy's Pizza Parlor had tried to give it a go after Poppy's death, but he just didn't have it in him to keep her namesake going. With much of the restaurant set up for our needs, I hoped it wouldn't require too much of an overhaul.

"Not many of these days left here," Uncle Jack said forlornly, shuffling his feet toward the kitchen. He seemed more upset Linda was moving away than me, but I would take that.

I took off my apron and hung it on the hook. "We're not going that far. And we'll still need you to sample our wares," I said. "You might see more of us than you do now." I headed to the coffee pot to brew another round.

Linda and Unkie smiled at each other. I would do everything I could to keep that flame alive and fan it whenever possible.

"Why don't we take a coffee break?" I suggested. They followed me to the corner next to the checkout counter. Linda and I had both brought our kittens to work today. Along with Unkie's kitten, and their father Willie, they raced around the room playing hide and seek. I couldn't imagine my life without my Peanut. She was both affectionate and playful. At home in my cottage when I had a rare moment of peace to read a book, she sat on my lap, her purr filling the quiet of the room.

I looked around, soaking in every memory I had made with Unkie since moving to Belle Harbor. My dream of a bakery of my own had been launched by him and was now moving to a new phase of business. I only hoped I could keep up with the demand. A small bakery in the corner of the antique shop was one thing. A full-fledged operation with a cafe was on a whole other level.

"How does *Luna's Bakery and Cafe* sound?" I asked. My grandma Luna was a woman before her time. She had owned her own business and forged her own way when women were still to be seen and not heard. She didn't give a darn for society's norms. She proudly set her own path, despite all of the naysayers. And by all accounts there were many, including both of my parents. For me to be following her footsteps was going to significantly ruffle feathers. But my gut and my heart said it was right.

I reached over and picked up my little Peanut as she attempted to escape under my chair.

Linda and Uncle Jack looked at each other. What was that about? Unkie laughed. "That's exactly what I guessed you'd name it," he said. "I'm really proud of you."

I put my fidgety little Peanut back on the floor to resume racing around with her siblings. I filled three cups with coffee and handed them out. "I'm as ready as I'm ever going to be. So I just need to go for it," I said. Constant encouragement and support from Uncle Jack to follow my dreams had prompted me to sign the lease on Poppy's. His faith in me was evidenced by co-signing on my loan for the renovations. Now the real work began.

We were just days away from a visit by my parents. It had been some time since I had spoken to them. I cradled the coffee cup, sipping the hot liquid. The only sound in the shop was the scurrying of kittens across the floor. My parents had taken the first step to reach out after I had left Boston to ask about a visit. I hoped with all my heart that it went well. I felt like I had let them down. Their vision for my life turned out to be a disaster. And somehow I blamed myself for things that were not my responsibility. Slowly, I was unburdening myself with the guilt. The time and distance helped.

Dad offered to help me with planning the renovations at Poppy's. I looked forward to partnering with him and taking advantage of his expertise as an architect and builder. His forte was large office buildings, so I hoped my teeny little cafe would be a breeze for him. And Mom offered to help design the cafe interior with her decorating touch.

This would either be the biggest disaster on earth or could be the beginning of repairing our relationships. I desperately hoped for the latter. No matter how old a girl got, she still needed her parents. I didn't want to get ahead of myself. One step at a time.

"I'm pretty excited about all of it," I said. "To new beginnings." I held up my cup, as they both did. In the corner of the room sat boxes still filled with the trains Unkie had bought from Linda at her estate sale.

I pointed. "Speaking of."

Linda's and Uncle Jack's gaze followed the direction of my arm. "I know," Unkie said.

"You still have those?" Linda asked.

"I'm torn. I know I could get quite a bit for the set. But there's just something about them that I can't part with." He headed to a box and pulled out one of the trains, showing us the piece.

"I've got an idea," I said, looking at both of them, grinning widely. "Why don't we take that train trip Linda suggested?" I shivered, not sure where that feeling came from.

"Oh, you mean the Coast Excursion?" Linda asked. She looked at Jack. "Say yes. You'll love it."

Unkie looked back and forth between us, slapping his knee. "I knew the two of you together was a bad idea. Tag teaming me."

"Well?" I asked.

He stood. "I would love nothing more than an adventure with two of my favorite people."

Linda clapped her hands. "I think they run it once a month. Sometimes they have themes, like stopping at a winery. They let you off for a tour, then another train picks you up on the way back to return home. The scenery is phenomenal. You can see the entire coastline on one side and greenery and mountains on the other."

"You two just tell me when and where to show up. I'm all in," Unkie said.

This was getting good.

CHAPTER FIFTEEN

Getting back to a routine after the nightmare catering event was a welcome experience. Linda and I had developed a system where we could produce our orders in about half the time it had taken me as a solo baker. Even though we were efficient, it was blatantly clear that the small kitchen in the corner of Uncle Jack's Checkered Past Antiques shop was no longer serving the need. The kindness and generosity of Unkie to carve out a space for me was unparalleled.

Making the decision to move to my own place was bittersweet. Thankfully, we weren't moving far down the boardwalk. The owner of Poppy's Pizza Parlor had tried to give it a go after Poppy's death, but he just didn't have it in him to keep her namesake going. With much of the restaurant set up for our needs, I hoped it wouldn't require too much of an overhaul.

"Not many of these days left here," Uncle Jack said forlornly, shuffling his feet toward the kitchen. He seemed more upset Linda was moving away than me, but I would take that.

I took off my apron and hung it on the hook. "We're not going that far. And we'll still need you to sample our wares," I said. "You might see more of us than you do now." I headed to the coffee pot to brew another round.

Linda and Unkie smiled at each other. I would do everything I could to keep that flame alive and fan it whenever possible.

"Why don't we take a coffee break?" I suggested. They followed me to the corner next to the checkout counter. Linda and I had both brought our kittens to work today. Along with Unkie's kitten, and their father Willie, they raced around the room playing hide and seek. I couldn't imagine my life without my Peanut. She was both affectionate and playful. At home in my cottage when I had a rare moment of peace to read a book, she sat on my lap, her purr filling the quiet of the room.

I looked around, soaking in every memory I had made with Unkie since moving to Belle Harbor. My dream of a bakery of my own had been launched by him and was now moving to a new phase of business.

I only hoped I could keep up with the demand. A small bakery in the corner of the antique shop was one thing. A full-fledged operation with a cafe was on a whole other level.

"How does *Luna's Bakery and Cafe* sound?" I asked. My grandma Luna was a woman before her time. She had owned her own business and forged her own way when women were still to be seen and not heard. She didn't give a darn for society's norms. She proudly set her own path, despite all of the naysayers. And by all accounts there were many, including both of my parents. For me to be following her footsteps was going to significantly ruffle feathers. But my gut and my heart said it was right.

I reached over and picked up my little Peanut as she attempted to escape under my chair.

Linda and Uncle Jack looked at each other. What was that about? Unkie laughed. "That's exactly what I guessed you'd name it," he said. "I'm really proud of you."

I put my fidgety little Peanut back on the floor to resume racing around with her siblings. I filled three cups with coffee and handed them out. "I'm as ready as I'm ever going to be. So I just need to go for it," I said. Constant encouragement and support from Uncle Jack to follow my dreams had prompted me to sign the lease on Poppy's.

His faith in me was evidenced by co-signing on my loan for the renovations. Now the real work began.

We were just days away from a visit by my parents. It had been some time since I had spoken to them. I cradled the coffee cup, sipping the hot liquid. The only sound in the shop was the scurrying of kittens across the floor. My parents had taken the first step to reach out after I had left Boston to ask about a visit. I hoped with all my heart that it went well. I felt like I had let them down. Their vision for my life turned out to be a disaster. And somehow I blamed myself for things that were not my responsibility. Slowly, I was unburdening myself with the guilt. The time and distance helped.

Dad offered to help me with planning the renovations at Poppy's. I looked forward to partnering with him and taking advantage of his expertise as an architect and builder. His forte was large office buildings, so I hoped my teeny little cafe would be a breeze for him. And Mom offered to help design the cafe interior with her decorating touch.

This would either be the biggest disaster on earth or could be the beginning of repairing our relationships. I desperately hoped for the latter. No matter how old a girl got, she still needed her parents. I didn't want to get ahead of myself. One step at a time.

"I'm pretty excited about all of it," I said. "To new beginnings." I held up my cup, as they both did. In the corner of the room sat boxes still filled with the trains Unkie had bought from Linda at her estate sale.

I pointed. "Speaking of."

Linda's and Uncle Jack's gaze followed the direction of my arm. "I know," Unkie said.

"You still have those?" Linda asked.

"I'm torn. I know I could get quite a bit for the set. But there's just something about them that I can't part with." He headed to a box and pulled out one of the trains, showing us the piece.

"I've got an idea," I said, looking at both of them, grinning widely. "Why don't we take that train trip Linda suggested?" I shivered, not sure where that feeling came from.

"Oh, you mean the Coast Excursion?" Linda asked. She looked at Jack. "Say yes. You'll love it."

Unkie looked back and forth between us, slapping his knee. "I knew the two of you together was a bad idea. Tag teaming me."

"Well?" I asked.

He stood. "I would love nothing more than an adventure with two of my favorite people."

Linda clapped her hands. "I think they run it once a month. Sometimes they have themes, like stopping at a winery. They let you off for a tour, then another train picks you up on the way back to return home. The scenery is phenomenal. You can see the entire coastline on one side and greenery and mountains on the other."

"You two just tell me when and where to show up. I'm all in," Unkie said.

This was getting good.

What's Next? Pies and Pandemonium

A *pie to die for, tangled family ties, and farmer's market folly...*

Sixth in the Belle Harbor Cozy Mystery series!

Buoyed by a new baking alliance with her business neighbor, Tilly teams up with her to enter the annual berry pie competition. Coupled with her parents first visit to quaint Belle Harbor, Tilly's got her plate full. No sooner does she reconnect with her mom, than a dead body inserts itself front and center.

With the death of his father, the heir apparent to the ceramic pie plate empire is prime suspect number one. But as Tilly, and her unlikely sleuthing partner mom team up to investigate, they quickly find layers of deception buried deep in the history of the annual pie competition.

Tilly and her mom reveal the length contestants will go to for the top prize in the contest. Can they slice up this juicy mystery to serve up the killer or will they be forced to eat humble pie?

Get Pies and Pandemonium from Amazon and start reading right away!

SNEAK PEEK OF PIES AND PANDEMONIUM

From the corner of my eye, I saw Mom quickly returning to our booth. She wildly waved one arm while continuing to clutch her purse close to her body. "Tilly, come quick! I think I saw a dead body!" she screamed.

I glanced at Florence and then around at the other contestants preparing their pies. All eyes were directed toward my mom. She must be mistaken. Mom continued toward us, tiptoeing quickly in her heels. As she panted, she said, "Over there, behind the booth." She turned and pointed in the direction of Mocha Joe's.

I came around to the outside of the booth and put my arm around her.

She slightly bent over, trying to catch her breath. "Tilly, you have to come back home to Boston now. It's just too dangerous for you here," she said.

One of the contestants brought a chair for Mom and she plopped into it, fanning her face. She held out her hand in a halting gesture. "Go find your father. He'll know what to do," she ordered.

I looked around, unsure what to do. What could she have seen that looked like a dead body? It must be her worrying about me that has caused a figment of her imagination to appear.

I put my hand on her shoulder as she bent over like she was going to hurl. "I'm sure it was nothing Mom," I said.

She whipped her head up and turned toward me, her eyebrows pinched together. "Tilly, I know what I saw. A man laying down. He had something like that smashed all around him." Mom pointed toward the pies lined up on the table.

"You mean a pie?" I asked. Every contestant had gathered around, listening to my mom regale us with her story. A few mumbles emanated from the crowd with confusion and disbelief. I was among them, not having a clue what she was explaining to me.

"Yes, Tilly," Mom sniffled, shaking her head, unable to continue.

Florence stepped forward and said, "Why don't you go with her to see what's happening. I'll be fine here."

I scanned the crowd, all eyes on us. Likely the only way to calm my mother down was to investigate and debunk her tale. I clasped Mom's hand and lifted her from the chair. "Oh, Tilly," she said and collapsed into my arms. I patted her back and gazed around at our audience.

"It's OK. Let's go see. We'll try to find dad on our way," I said. Up until now my parent's visit had been relatively drama free. Except, you know, the usual. I deeply hoped this was not going to turn into something of a major incident. But it had all indications that would be the case. Squeezing Mom's hand I led her from our booth. The sun had begun to heat up the pavement of the parking lot in the market, radiating warmth. I removed my sweater and tied it around my waist.

Mom lifted her arm, indicating the direction of her concern. Up ahead, Unkie and Linda chatted up customer's at Mocha Joe's booth as they served the coffee and scones. It didn't appear they had any concern about a body that might be nearby. Mom stepped forward and turned right down a path that wound behind the booths toward the restrooms. Ceramics World was on our left. And Litton Berry Farms was on our right. The customer line for snapping up those berries was just as long as the line for coffee. It was prime time for those little gems, and the locals stocked up to make their berry goodies.

I glimpsed into the ceramic booth, not seeing anyone there. The owner of the business wouldn't be far. Terry's pie plates were the go to for the contestants. And his work permeated throughout the town, most restaurants buying many sets of dishes from him.

Mom abruptly stopped before we entered the alleyway, covering her mouth with one hand and pointing with the other, her eyes wide open. I craned my neck, but didn't see anything out of order. I held up my arm for her to stay put while I looked. How could there be a body so close to the action with nobody else except my mom noticing it? I advanced to the opening and turned left, seeing Terry in full display. He was laid out with what appeared to be a berry pie smashed in pieces laying near his head.

Mom edged next to me. "See?" she whispered.

I did see. And it was not good. I crouched and put a finger on the top of Terry's foot, checking for a pulse. Nothing. Not good at all.

Get Pies and Pandemonium from Amazon and start reading right away!

About The Author

Sue Hollowell is a wife and empty nester with a lot of mom left over. Finding a lot of time on her hands, and as a lover of mystery novels, she began telling the story of a character who appeared in her head.

The Chemical Bond is a book about Meredith Markette, a young woman who reluctantly enters into the field of law enforcement when her police officer father is killed in the line of duty. Her quest is to discover his murderer and in the meantime come to terms with a tragedy of her youth.

Will this book ever see the light of day? Maybe. Sue really likes the story and character. And writing that book taught her a ton about the publishing industry. Through this experience she has discovered a love of writing stories, and especially mysteries. She hopes you enjoy her books as much as she enjoys writing them.

Connect with Sue on Facebook at www.facebook.com/sueh ollowellauthor and sign up for her newsletter to stay in touch with all things cozy!